The
PRIN
DIARIES

Diary 2005

belongs to

Princess emily rodgers

**If found, please contact Her
Royal Highness at**

Address: 6 Pearwood
Close, Tarporley,
Cheshire, CW6 0UF

Phone number: 01829
733659

Email: eric.rodgers@tesco.net

Meg Cabot is the author of many books for young adults, including the phenomenally successful *The Princess Diaries* series, *The Mediator* series, *All American Girl*, *Nicola and the Viscount* and *Victoria and the Rogue*, as well as several books for adult readers. Meg currently lives in New York City with her husband and one-eyed cat called Henrietta, and says she is still waiting for her real parents, the king and queen, to restore her to her rightful throne.

There are two Walt Disney Pictures feature films based on *The Princess Diaries*.

Visit Meg Cabot's website at *www.megcabot.co.uk*

Books about Princess Mia

The Princess Diaries
The Princess Diaries: Take Two
The Princess Diaries: Third Time Lucky
The Princess Diaries: Mia Goes Fourth
The Princess Diaries: Give Me Five
The Princess Diaries: Sixsational

The Princess Diaries Guide to Life
The Princess Diaries Princess Files
The Princess Diaries Mia's Christmas

The PRINCESS DIARIES

Diary 2005

Meg Cabot

Illustrated by Nicola Slater

MACMILLAN CHILDREN'S BOOKS

First published 2005 by Macmillan Children's Books
a division of Macmillan Publishers Limited
20 New Wharf Road, London N1 9RR
Basingstoke and Oxford
www.panmacmillan.com

Associated companies throughout the world

ISBN 0 330 42122 0

1 3 5 7 9 8 6 4 2

A CIP catalogue record for this book is available from
the British Library.

Typeset by Atomic Squib
Printed and bound in Great Britain by Mackays of Chatham plc, Kent

INTRODUCTION

By Her Royal Highness
Princess Mia Thermopolis

Being a princess isn't easy. I mean, it's hard enough to keep track of slumber parties, term paper due dates, babysitting gigs and soccer practices. Try throwing in coronations, ball-gown fittings, movie premieres with the royal consort and functions of state!

That's why I'm so glad I have this engagement diary to help keep my royal agenda straight. Without it, I swear I'd be completely lost! It's no joke trying to remember the birthdays of every single member of the palace housekeeping staff, let alone when the next Algebra review session has been scheduled! The last thing I need is a coup d'état or a C on a final.

But simply by jotting down in this little book what time the limo is coming or what's due when, I've managed to get control of my life at last. Sort of.

My Top Ten Hottest Guys

1. _____
2. _____
3. _____
4. _____
5. _____
6. _____
7. _____
8. _____
9. _____
10. _____

Comments: _____
_____
_____
_____
_____
_____
_____
_____

Ten Things I'd Do if I Were a Princess

1. _____
2. _____
3. _____
4. _____
5. _____
6. _____
7. _____
8. _____
9. _____
10. _____

Comments: _____

_____

_____

_____

_____

_____

_____

_____

January

My New Year's Resolutions for 2005

I will improve myself in the following ways:

1. _____
2. _____
3. _____

I will break the following bad habits:

1. biting my nails
2. _____
3. _____

I will not recriminate myself for failing to uphold the above resolutions. Instead, I will:

1. _____
2. _____
3. *Put on my tiara and know that I am a princess*

Improve (v.): to make better, to make more valuable
Do you think this extra credit will improve my Algebra grade?

FRIDAY *New Year's Eve*

31

SATURDAY *Happy New Year*

1

SUNDAY

2

Random Act of Princess

New Year's Day is a time of reflection. Make sure your
mirrors are sparkly clean by Windexing.

MONDAY *UK Bank Holiday*

3

TUESDAY *Bank Holiday in Scotland*

4

WEDNESDAY *Birthday of Michael Moscovitz*

5

THURSDAY *Epiphany*

6

FRIDAY
7
Recycle (v.): To convert for reuse
Mia recycled her old bootlaces by making a lovely
macramé bracelet for Lilly.

SATURDAY
8
Now is the perfect time to refresh your
wardrobe — everything is on sale!

SUNDAY
9

Random Act of Princess
Mia gives Michael a moon rock for his birthday. What old,
useless thing do you have that would make a nice gift for
someone? A plate from an old coat of armour or a picture
frame you've enamelled with nail varnish might make a
meaningful gift.

MONDAY
10
Spoiler (n.): illicitly gained information
pertaining to future television episodes or
upcoming feature films
Mia trolls the Internet for hours each week looking
for STAR WARS Episode III spoilers.

TUESDAY
11

WEDNESDAY
12

THURSDAY
13

FRIDAY
14

SATURDAY
15

SUNDAY
16

Random Act of Princess

Don't be left out of the loop! Google your favourite TV shows or upcoming movies along with the word spoilers and find out what's going to happen. Then email all your friends and tell them. They'll be eternally grateful, because there are enough problems in real life. Who needs surprises on your favourite show or in a highly anticipated movie?

January

MONDAY

17

TUESDAY _Birthday of Princess Claire of Belgium_

18

WEDNESDAY

19

THURSDAY

20

Princess Aquarius (20 January–19 February): changeable, talented, inquisitive. Does your monarchy need royal adjustment? You're a reformer, Aquarius, so get going! Best royal consorts: Gemini, Libra.

Possible brief affaires de coeur: Aries, Sagittarius.

FRIDAY
Eid-ul-Adah (Muslim)

21

SATURDAY
Franc (n.): Unit of currency formerly used in France and Genovia
Grandmere was very confused when Genovia converted from the franc to the euro.

22

SUNDAY
Birthday of Princess Caroline of Monaco

23

Random Act of Princess

Have you opened your own bank account yet? Now is the time to begin saving for that spring-break bikini.

MONDAY
24

TUESDAY
25

Appropriate (adj.): suitable, proper
Lilly's royal-blue nails were not appropriate for
her meeting with the deputy mayor.

WEDNESDAY
26

Bikinis are not appropriate
swimwear for crown princesses.

THURSDAY
27

Holocaust Memorial Day

FRIDAY
28

SATURDAY
29

You're never too old for winter fun. If you live in a cold climate and are lucky enough to have snow, organize a snowball fight or a sledge race. Don't forget the mini marshmallows in your hot cocoa!

SUNDAY
30

Random Act of Princess

Liven up the end of January by wearing bright colours — but PLEASE don't forget to change into something more appropriate for your princess lessons.

January

MONDAY

31

Notes

February

MONDAY
31

TUESDAY
1
Birthday of Meg Cabot
Birthday of Princess Stephanie of Monaco

WEDNESDAY
2

THURSDAY
3
Decree (n.): an order given having the force of law
The latest decree from the Genovian Parliament concerns the installation of public parking meters.

FRIDAY

4

SATURDAY
Race (n.): a contest of speed
The latest race was a locker-to-cafeteria obstacle
course.

5

SUNDAY

6

Random Act of Princess

February is the shortest month, but it often feels like the longest.
Entertain yourself by cutting your time on all sorts of activities —
see how short you can make your shower, or how quickly you
can get to school (without letting your chauffeur speed).
Making a race out of anything can be fun. Pointless, but fun.

February

MONDAY
7
In the days leading up to Lent, Genovians celebrate Carnivale by dancing in the streets, depriving themselves of nothing, and drinking Poire William (made from Genovian pears, of course).

TUESDAY
8
Shrove Tuesday (Pancake Day!)

WEDNESDAY
9
Chinese New Year (Year of the Rooster)
Ash Wednesday/ (Lent begins)

THURSDAY
10
Deprive (v.): take away from
Boris is reluctant to retire to the supply closet to practise his violin, as it will deprive others of the pleasure of listening to him play.

FRIDAY
11

SATURDAY
12

SUNDAY
13

Random Act of Princess

Time to start planning (if you haven't already) what you're going to give your Valentine. Some royal ideas include:
• Movie passes for two • Any LORD OF THE RINGS DVD, preferably the extended version • A wire-less router

MONDAY *St Valentine's Day*

14

TUESDAY

15

WEDNESDAY *Cadeau (n.): gift*
I received a lovely cadeau from my royal consort.

16

THURSDAY

17

FRIDAY
18

SATURDAY
19

SUNDAY
20

Princess Pisces (19 February–20 March):
sensitive, romantic, self-sacrificing.
You always do what you can to help, Pisces,
whether it's political support or a nail file.
Best royal consorts: Cancer, Scorpio.
Possible brief affaires de coeur: Taurus, Capricorn.

Random Act of Princess

Valentine's Day is not just about receiving a cadeau from a
beau! Share the love by passing out Valentines to all your
subjects.

February

MONDAY *President's Day, USA*

21

TUESDAY

22

WEDNESDAY

23

THURSDAY

24

FRIDAY
25
Prom (n.): traditional spring high-school dance
Mia and Michael disagree over the appeal of attending the prom.

SATURDAY
26

SUNDAY
27

Random Act of Princess

It might seem like spring is a long way away, but it's really just around the corner. Now is the time to start shopping for a prom dress if you don't want to have to choose from icky picked-over ones that are left by the time your royal consort finally asks you to go with him.

MONDAY
28

Notes

March

March is in like a lion, out like a lamb!

TUESDAY *St David's Day*

1 *Only _____ more days until the end Of the term!*

WEDNESDAY

2

THURSDAY *Cumulonimbus (n.): a storm cloud*

3 *They planned a picnic despite the overlarge Cumulonimbus hovering in the sky.*

FRIDAY
4
Birthday of Grandmere

What do you get for the woman who has everything? One can never have too many padded satin clothes hangers.

SATURDAY
5

SUNDAY
6
Mothering Sunday

Whether or not your mother is a free-spirited artist, a former supermodel or a Freudian psychoanalyst, she's something special because she's yours. Do something special for her, like taking her to tea at the Plaza. Or at least fixing her some Lipton with fudge-striped cookies.

Random Act of Princess

Make up a haiku using very March words, like cumulonimbus, daffodil and chilly. Example:

    Cumulonimbus
    Like lacy daffodils float
    Through a chilly sky

March

MONDAY

7

TUESDAY *International Women's Day*

8

WEDNESDAY *Only _____ days left until the end of term!*

9

THURSDAY

10

FRIDAY
11

Power (n.): the product of a number multiplied by itself
36 is the power of 6.

SATURDAY
12

SUNDAY
13

Random Act of Princess

No one's arguing that passing notes in class isn't mentally stimulating. However, it is International Women's Week. Prove your feminine power and your smarts by studying up.

MONDAY

14

TUESDAY
Beware the Ides of March. (Um, hello, if
you don't get this, you really should read
Shakespeare's JULIUS CAESAR. Michael has — three
times).

15

WEDNESDAY

16

THURSDAY *St Patrick's Day*

17

FRIDAY
18

Did you know that on the vernal and autumnal equinoxes, if you balance an egg on its end, it will stand up by itself? This is because of mysterious equatorial forces. Try it and see!

SATURDAY
19

SUNDAY
20

Vernal equinox
Palm Sunday

Random Act of Princess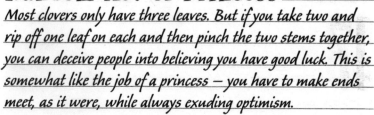

Most clovers only have three leaves. But if you take two and rip off one leaf on each and then pinch the two stems together, you can deceive people into believing you have good luck. This is somewhat like the job of a princess — you have to make ends meet, as it were, while always exuding optimism.

MONDAY *Princess Aries (21 March—20 April):*

21 *responsible, dynamic, dominant.*

If you lead, Aries, the people will follow. Lead them to wise choices, fashion included.

Best royal consorts: Leo, Sagittarius.

Possible brief affaires de coeur: Gemini, Aquarius.

TUESDAY

22

WEDNESDAY *Birthday of Princess Eugenie of England*

23

THURSDAY *Batik (n.): method of printing patterns*

24 *by waxing portions not to be dyed*

Ling Su used batik to make her beautiful purple-and-white egg.

FRIDAY
25
Good Friday

SATURDAY
26

SUNDAY
27
Easter Day

British Summer Time begins — remember, spring forward, fall back

Random Act of Princess

Easter is about many things to many people, but one of the most widely accepted practices during this holiday is colouring eggs. From simple PAAS kits to Grandmere's favourites by Fabergé to elaborate Martha Stewart-esque eggstravaganzas involving wax pens, live it up. If your egg creation is meant to last, do be sure to empty it, however.

MONDAY *Easter Monday*

28

TUESDAY

29

WEDNESDAY *April Fool's Day is the day after tomorrow — get your prank plans in order!*

30

THURSDAY *Can't afford a spring-break trip to Florida this year? Don't despair! make your own beach by turning up the heat and walking around the house in flip-flops and shorts. Don't forget the sunscreen!*

31

April

It's April Fool's Day, and you're still without a princessy plan? Choose one of the following royal pranks, guaranteed to con even the cleverest courtier:

· Tell your royal consort you'll be moving to your country to rule, pronto

· Make up a story and tell it like it really happened

· Tell your favourite lady-in-waiting her shoelaces are untied

· Choose the most unlikely, unappealing hobby (like collecting medical oddity photos) and tell your parents, the king and queen, you are now an enthusiast

There are many other much more clever activities you can engage in on this Day of the Fool, but these will do in a pinch.

FRIDAY *April Fool's Day*

1

SATURDAY *Fool (n.): one who behaves unwisely*
Boris is a fool for Lilly.

2

SUNDAY

3

Random Act of Princess

Whatever trickery you engage in, make sure you don't let 1 April end before you tell your victim the truth!

April

MONDAY

4

TUESDAY

5

Spring fever (n.): a lazy, restless feeling
associated with the coming of spring
The April breeze floating in through the window
gave Fat Louie spring fever.

WEDNESDAY

6

THURSDAY

7

April

FRIDAY
8

SATURDAY
9

SUNDAY
10

Random Act of Princess

Spring is almost here! Paint your toenails a beautiful pastel to celebrate the coming season: robin's-egg blue, mint green, lemon yellow, lavender and, of course, pale pink. Give yourself a royally good pedicure while you're at it, especially if your toes haven't seen the light of day for five or six months.

April

MONDAY
11

Persevere (v.): to continue steadfastly, especially under unpleasant circumstances

Mia perseveres through both Algebra and princess lessons.

TUESDAY
12

WEDNESDAY
13

THURSDAY
14

FRIDAY
15
Day of Perseverance, Genovia

SATURDAY
16
In 1291, Princess Thérése persevered in her plan to have sewers dug from the palace to the Bay of Genovia.

SUNDAY
17

Random Act of Princess
Princesses don't complain, they persevere.
There are this many days until the end of the school year:

April

MONDAY 18

Squander (v.): to spend wastefully
Tina squanders her time reading romance novels.
But she thoroughly enjoys herself.

TUESDAY 19

WEDNESDAY 20

THURSDAY 21

Birthday of Queen Elizabeth II of England
Princess Taurus (21 April–21 May): productive,
tolerant, patient.
It isn't easy running a kingdom, Taurus, but
nobody vanquishes bureaucracy like you!
Best royal consorts: Virgo, Capricorn.
Possible brief affaires de coeur: Cancer, Pisces.

FRIDAY *Earth Day*

22

SATURDAY *St George's Day*
Passover begins at sundown

23

SUNDAY

24

Random Act of Princess

Earth Day is an important reminder that you will never reach self-actualization at the rate at which you're squandering paper. Use the back!

April

MONDAY
25

TUESDAY
26

WEDNESDAY
27

THURSDAY
28
Birthday of Princess Rosagunde of Genovia

April

FRIDAY
29

SATURDAY
30
Frock (n.): dress or gown
Grandmere insisted Mia wear a pink frock to the prom.

SUNDAY
1

Random Act of Princess

Cleanliness is next to royalness: Give the regal boudoir a thorough spring-cleaning. Time to put away those bulky sweaters and take out your spring party frocks.

Notes

May

May Day is a time of celebration, mostly with flowers*, but always with a sense of giddy abandonment (see Guinevere's number entitled 'The Lusty Month of May' in the musical *Camelot* for a good illustration of this). On May Day, consider some of the following ways to celebrate the day:

· Substitute your tiara with a wreath of flowers and wear it all day long
· Set up a maypole in your garden or a local park (be sure to check if a permit is needed!), festoon with flowers and ribbons, and dance, dance, dance!
· Learn Morse code for 'Mayday'
· Pull out every item of clothing you own with a flower pattern on it and wear as much of it as you can together, all at once. If you persuade your ladies-in-waiting to do the same you will not look as foolish
· Learn how to say 'May' in several different languages Here's a start: Mayo (Spanish), Mai (French)
· Make a number of small bouquets and offer them, willy-nilly, to those you encounter

Flower (n.): the best part of something
G&T is the *flower* of Mia's schedule.

*Please remember that obtaining flowers from a neighbour's garden or a municipal building without permission is frowned upon.

May

FRIDAY
29

SATURDAY
30

SUNDAY
1
May Day
Birthday of Princess Mia

Random Act of Princess

One last idea, only to be implemented after considering your
pet's disposition and/or claws: place a wreath on your pet's
head, or in lieu of a collar. Resting blooms on top of the
aquarium will do too!

May

MONDAY
2
May Bank Holiday

Special (adj.): exceptional in quality

Fat Louie is a special cat.

TUESDAY
3

WEDNESDAY
4

THURSDAY
5
Ascension Day

FRIDAY

6

SATURDAY

7

SUNDAY

8

Random Act of Princess

Invent your own royal act here:

May

MONDAY

9

TUESDAY *Birthday of Rocky Thermopolis-Gianini*

10

WEDNESDAY

11

THURSDAY *Horror (n.): a feeling of fear and loathing*
Lana's jaw dropped in horror when she heard who Josh was taking to the Cultural Diversity Dance.

12

May

FRIDAY *Friday the 13th!*
13

SATURDAY
14

SUNDAY
15

Random Act of Princess

Friday the 13th is really the ideal time to grab your consort and take in a horror flick so you can sit next to him, share popcorn and grab his arm during the scary parts. Just don't forget the Milk Duds!

May

MONDAY *Promulgate (v.): announce publicly*
16 *In 1812, Princess Anne Claire promulgated the first Genovian Constitution.*

TUESDAY
17

WEDNESDAY *Genovian Constitution Day*
18

THURSDAY
19

FRIDAY
20
Genovian Constitution Day celebrated

SATURDAY
21
Princess Gemini (May 21–June 22):
clever, charming, flexible
Gemini, you're extra easy to work with on matters
of state — you're smart and versatile!
Best royal consorts: Libra, Aquarius
Possible brief affaires de coeur: Aries, Leo

SUNDAY
22

Random Act of Princess

Are chores in your house promulgated and subsequently
assigned? If not, make up a nifty new work chart (using
pieces of coloured felt on Velcro) to divide the household tasks
fairly between your siblings/housemates. They will be sure to
appreciate your princessy proactiveness.

May

MONDAY *Victoria Day, Canada*

23

TUESDAY

24

WEDNESDAY *Celebrate (v.): to honour with*
festivities
Mia celebrated her birthday by having a party at
the Loft.

25

THURSDAY

26

FRIDAY
27

SATURDAY
28

SUNDAY
29

Random Act of Princess

Queen Victoria's birthday — 24 May — is celebrated every year on the penultimate Monday of May in Canada. Think about what kind of activities would be fun when your birthday is declared a national holiday!

MONDAY
UK Spring Bank Holiday

Memorial Day

30
It is now OK to break out the white trousers and shoes!

TUESDAY

31

Notes

June

June is Genovian History Month. The region that is now called Genovia has been inhabited by humans since the Ice Age, 30,000 years ago. One can still find cave paintings in and around the cliffs along the Genovian coastline. Significant events in Genovian history include St Amelie's heroic measures in the face of invading forces in 1084 and Princess Agnes's act of defiance culminating in love in 1716. No event is more significant than that commemorated by June's Rosagunde Day, however.

WEDNESDAY

1

THURSDAY *Rosagunde Day, Genovia*

2

June

FRIDAY
3

Marauder (n.): one who raids for plunder Genovian princess Rosagunde is forever a heroine to her countrymen and women for protecting her land against marauders, including the Visigoth Alboin, whom she strangled with her braid.

SATURDAY
4

SUNDAY
5

Random Act of Princess

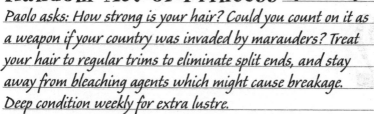

Paolo asks: How strong is your hair? Could you count on it as a weapon if your country was invaded by marauders? Treat your hair to regular trims to eliminate split ends, and stay away from bleaching agents which might cause breakage. Deep condition weekly for extra lustre.

MONDAY

6

TUESDAY

7

Swim (v.): float or be supported on water Genovian beaches are famous for swimming and toplessness.

WEDNESDAY

8

Feast of Princess Agnes, Genovia

THURSDAY

9

FRIDAY
10

Though she couldn't swim, Princess Agnes of Genovia threw herself off the Pont de Vierges rather than enter a convent in 1716. She was fished out by a passing sailor, whom she married and bore fourteen children.

SATURDAY
11

SUNDAY
12

Random Act of Princess

Summertime means swimwear! Have you found a suit to match your royal body type?
- *Big on top should look for plenty of support*
- *Big on the bottom should look for high-cut legs*
- *Straight up and down should look for bold patterns*

June

MONDAY

13

TUESDAY

14

WEDNESDAY

15

THURSDAY *Royal (adj.): worthy of a king or queen*
(or princess)

16 *Grandmere considers the Sidecar a royal drink.*

FRIDAY
17

SATURDAY
18

SUNDAY *Father's Day*
19

Even if he isn't a crown prince, tell Dad thanks. You know, for the whole fathering-you thing. Lipton tea and fudge-striped cookies might come in handy here too.

Random Act of Princess

Going to camp this summer? Bring a new address book with you and pass it around the campfire with a pen. You'll get your new friends' screen names so you can IM them after you part ways at the end. Be sure to add their snail-mail addresses to the royal mailing list!

MONDAY
20

TUESDAY
21
Summer solstice
Birthday of Prince William of England

WEDNESDAY
22
Princess Cancer (22 June–23 July):
intuitive, imaginative, magnetic.
Royal flattery doesn't fool you, Cancer — you know
who your court allies are.
Best royal consorts: Scorpio, Pisces.
Possible brief affaires de coeur: Taurus, Virgo.

THURSDAY
23

FRIDAY
24

SATURDAY
25

Fairy (n.): an imaginary small being supposed to have magical powers
Tinkerbell is a fairy.

SUNDAY
26

Random Act of Princess

Summer solstice — you know what that means! Oh. You don't? Well, who really does? Just be sure to take a hint from the unfortunates in A MIDSUMMER NIGHT'S DREAM and know who you might fall in love with if the fairies find you wandering in the woods.

June

MONDAY
27

Have you been wearing sunscreen? Make sure you have, because it is not glamorous to look like an old leather bag by the time you're thirty.

TUESDAY
28

WEDNESDAY
29

THURSDAY
30

July

In honour of Canada Day and US and Genovian Independence Days, here are Mia's seven basic types of government:

· Anarchy: absence of government
· Monarchy: government where supreme power is in the hands of one person
· Aristocracy: government vested in those most distinguished by birth or fortune
· Dictatorship: government of absolute authority
· Oligarchy: government by a few persons or family
· Democracy: government by the people
· Principality: government by a prince or princess (no king or queen)

Genovia is a principality.

FRIDAY

1

Canada Day, Canada

Birthday of Princess Diana of England

SATURDAY

2

Federation (n.): a federated society or group of states

In 1867, Canada became a federation.

SUNDAY

3

Random Act of Princess

Celebrate Canada Day! Wear a maple leaf, think fondly of ice hockey, or just be glad that in 1867 the provinces joined together as one federation.

July

MONDAY *Independence Day, USA*

4

TUESDAY

5

WEDNESDAY *Independence (n.): not bound or*
subject to another
Mia does not have independence from Grandmere.

6

THURSDAY

7

FRIDAY
8

Revolution (n.): forcible overthrow of a political system
For Mia to be free of her princess lessons, a revolution would have to take place.

SATURDAY
9

SUNDAY
10

Random Act of Princess

Hold a royal fireworks display in honour of American Independence Day. Be warned, however: sparklers and fireworks are exciting and pretty, but highly dangerous and mostly illegal if not sponsored by a licensed company. Fire pretty, burn bad.
The only time it is acceptable for a princess to be hauled off by the police is in circumstances of revolution.

MONDAY *Genovian Independence Day*

11

TUESDAY *Battle of the Boyne*

12

WEDNESDAY

13

THURSDAY *Birthday of Crown Princess Victoria of Sweden*

14

FRIDAY
15

Sparkle (v.): glitter, twinkle
The Royal Genovian jewels sparkle like nothing
else.

SATURDAY
16

SUNDAY
17

Random Act of Princess

Throw your own Genovian Independence Day celebration:
Invite your friends to a sumptuous feast of Genovian olives
and pears. Don't forget Genovian sparkling cider. Encourage
everyone to dress in the colours of the Genovian flag (blue, gold
and white).

July

MONDAY
18
Lull (v.): induce calmness in

In 1084, Amelie, patron saint of Genovia, lulled an Italian count intent on pillaging her country to sleep by singing traditional Genovian folksongs, then cut off his head with a meat cleaver.

TUESDAY
19

WEDNESDAY
20

THURSDAY
21
Feast of St Amelie, Genovia

FRIDAY

22

SATURDAY

23

SUNDAY

24

Princess Leo (24 July–23 August):
authoritative, creative, proud
Leo, you were born to rule. Everyone looks up to
you, and you never disappoint.
Best royal consorts: Aries, Sagittarius.
Possible brief affaires de coeur: Gemini, Libra.

Random Act of Princess

Memorize the lyrics to as many songs (everything from
Broadway musicals to Top 40) as you can. You never know
when you might need to perform one as karaoke or to lull an
enemy to sleep.

MONDAY *Fry (v.): boil in oil*

25

Princess Bernadette's refusal to marry Italian governor Barbera resulted in a ninety-day siege, ending only when Bernadette ordered boiling olive oil be poured from palace walls on to the governor's army, which fled lest it be fried.

TUESDAY *Freedom Day, Genovia*

26

WEDNESDAY

27

THURSDAY

28

FRIDAY

29

SATURDAY *Birthday of Lilly Moscovitz*

30

SUNDAY

31

Random Act of Princess

Have you found a summer job? No job is beneath a princess needing pocket money with which to embellish her autumn wardrobe. Employment in food services (such as fry cook) can lead to leadership opportunities elsewhere (just don't tell your friends where you work if you don't like how you look in your uniform).

Notes

August

August

MONDAY _Bank Holiday (Scotland)_

1

TUESDAY _Dog Days (n.): hottest days of summer,
generally in August
Pavlov rides out the dog days of summer in the
air-conditioned Moscovitz apartment_

2

WEDNESDAY

3

THURSDAY

4

FRIDAY
5

SATURDAY
6

SUNDAY
7

Random Act of Princess

Remember that humans aren't the only ones who like air conditioning. As we enter the dog days of summer, remember our four-legged friends. Make sure the royal pets have plenty of water and shade.

August

MONDAY *Birthday of Princess Beatrice of England*

8

TUESDAY

9

WEDNESDAY

10

THURSDAY

11

FRIDAY

12

Paraphernalia (n.): personal belongings or accessories

Lilly's paraphernalia from the Anger Management concert she attended includes her ticket stub, 1 ripped T-shirt (possibly containing drops of Jacoby Shaddix's perspiration), and temporary deafness.

SATURDAY

13

SUNDAY

14

Random Act of Princess

What has been the best part of this summer for you? Collect paraphernalia associated with this event (whether it's shells from the Genovian shore or tickets from that marathon concert) and put it together in a scrapbook for yourself.

August

MONDAY *Birthday of Princess Anne of England*

15

TUESDAY

16

WEDNESDAY

17

THURSDAY *Birthday of Crown Prince Philippe of Genovia*

18

FRIDAY
19

Member (n.): one part of a complex whole
In 1990, Genovia became a member of the UN.

SATURDAY
20

SUNDAY
21

Random Act of Princess

Time to start thinking about what extracurricular activities you'd like to take part in this coming school year. What about becoming a member of the drama club or hockey team? Joining student government? If the latter, why not start making campaign posters now while you have time? Stock up on glitter and if possible, diamanté from your grandmother's old Bob Mackie evening gowns.

August

MONDAY

22

TUESDAY

23

WEDNESDAY

24

Princess Virgo (24 August—
23 September): altruistic, dedicated, persuasive.
If it's foreign policy or a formal ball, you always get
what you want, Virgo.
Best royal consorts: Taurus, Capricorn.
Possible brief affaires de coeur: Cancer, Scorpio.

THURSDAY

25

FRIDAY
26
Integral (adj.): essential

A tiara is integral to a princess's wardrobe.

SATURDAY
27

SUNDAY
28

Random Act of Princess

Sebastiano says: The worst time of the year to sho* for back-to-school clothes is ri* before school starts. The best time to pur* integ* new pieces of your autumn war* is either after Christmas or during the autumn fash* previews. Princesses nev* pay retail — or they wear cout*.

*shop *right *purchase *integral *wardrobe *fashion *never *couture

August

MONDAY
29

UK Summer Bank Holiday

Dread (v.): anticipate with fear or loathing
Mia dreaded sophomore geometry.

TUESDAY
30

WEDNESDAY
31

Notes

September

It Ain't Over Till It's Over Summer
Barbecue Invitation

Dear _____

You are cordially invited to Your Highness
_____ 's final summer barbecue bash.
Do not fret: vegetarian cuisine will also be served.
Please meet at my
garden/roof/deck/patio/fire-escape,
on ____ of September 2005.
Follow the trail of smoke.

RSVP:_____

Most affectionately,
HRH_____

THURSDAY _____

1

September

FRIDAY
Necessary (adj.): essential
For back-to-school, new laces are necessary for
Mia's Doc Martens.

2

SATURDAY
Beginning of Ramadan

3

SUNDAY

4

Random Act of Princess
Royal list of absolutely necessary new school supplies:

MONDAY *Labor Day, USA*

No more white trousers or shoes! Unless you are a nurse.

5

TUESDAY

6

WEDNESDAY *The new TV season is starting up. Have you got your VCR or TiVo ready?*

7

THURSDAY

8

FRIDAY
9

SATURDAY
10

SUNDAY
11
Grandparents' Day

Remember the dowager princess in your life:
time once again to bust out the Lipton and
fudge-striped cookies.

Random Act of Princess

September nights can be nippy. Now is a good time to take
your winter things out of storage and start airing them out. A
princess never smells of mothballs.

MONDAY *Is back to school giving you the blues? Wear*
12 *a tiara to school for a week. Tell anyone who asks*
that you're practising for when your real parents,
the king and queen, come to get you.

TUESDAY
13

WEDNESDAY
14

THURSDAY *Birthday of Prince Henry (aka Harry)*
15 *of England*

FRIDAY
16

Antisocial (adj.): withdrawing oneself from others

Grandmere considers it antisocial of Mia to prefer a date with Michael over a royal ball.

SATURDAY
17

SUNDAY
18

Random Act of Princess

The new school year brings lots of opportunities, both academic and social. Invite a new student to join you and your group at lunch. If she doesn't end up fitting in, you'll have someone new to talk about.

MONDAY *Diary (n.): a daily record of events, especially*
those concerning the writer
19 *In the movie of her life, Mia's diary is red with a*
big gold lock.

TUESDAY

20

WEDNESDAY

21

THURSDAY *Birthday of Princess Martha Louise of*
Norway
22

FRIDAY
23
Autumnal equinox
Mia writes her first diary entry

SATURDAY
24
Princess Libra (24 September—23 October): artistic, rational, diplomatic. What's fair is fair, Libra, and you always know it. Very important for a princess! Best royal consorts: Gemini, Aquarius. Possible brief affaires de coeur: Leo, Sagittarius.

SUNDAY
25

Random Act of Princess
A diary is the perfect place to vent things like how unfair it is that your parents never told you that you were a princess, or that your best friend can sometimes be a little mean, or that you can't stand the way Judith Gershner is making eyes at the man of your dreams. Start a diary today!

September

MONDAY
26

TUESDAY
Olive Day, Genovia
27

WEDNESDAY
28

THURSDAY
Olive (n.): A small pitted fruit from
which oil is obtained
29
In 1004, the Royal Genovian Olive Press was
founded.

FRIDAY

30

Random Act of Princess

You don't have to settle for using gloppy school salad dressing in the cafeteria. Make your own and bring it to school in a bottle or a jar with a screw top (be sure you have access to a refrigerator if you have more than a day's supply). Mia's favourite salad dressing is:

1 part balsamic vinegar

3 parts olive oil (preferably Genovian*)

1 tsp mustard

salt and pepper

Shake well!

*Genovian olive oil is low in saturated fat and contains only good cholesterol.

Notes

Notes

October

October brings cool temperatures, falling leaves, pumpkins
and general spookiness. To capture the mood of the season,
try writing haikus using autumnal words like nip, candy and
freak show. Example:

> *It's Hallowe'en Eve*
> *Dress like a total freak show*
> *Nip all the candy*

or

> *The bitter wind nips*
> *I turn to yonder freak show*
> *Candy to my soul*

FRIDAY
30

SATURDAY
1

Shock (n.): a strong reaction of horror
Mia was shocked to learn her mother was dating
her Algebra teacher, never mind the fact that she
herself was a princess.

SUNDAY
2

The Day Mia Found Out She Was A Princess
(DMFOSWAP)

Random Act of Princess

Get out the crystal and toast your Tab to Mia, and to the
princess in us all.

MONDAY *Rosh Hashanah begins at sundown*

3

TUESDAY

4

WEDNESDAY *Classic (adj.): Of recognizable and unquestionable high quality*
DIRTY DANCING is a classic movie.

5

THURSDAY

6

FRIDAY _Birthday of Tina Hakim Baba_

7

SATURDAY _Repertoire (n.): A list of skills or ingredients_
Shameeka recently added cheerleading to her repertoire.

8

SUNDAY

9

Random Act of Princess

Go to a bookstore or library and pick up a classic novel by Jane Austen or one of the Brontë sisters. You'll be expanding your literary repertoire AND getting to read about hotties like Mr Rochester.

October

MONDAY *Columbus Day, USA*
Thanksgiving Day, Canada
10

TUESDAY
11

WEDNESDAY *Yom Kippur begins at sundown*
12

THURSDAY *The day Mia stabbed Lana with a nutty*
royale
13

FRIDAY 14

Vengeance (n.): act aimed at injuring someone who has injured oneself or one's friends
Via the nutty royale, Mia sought vengeance upon Lana for the wrongs done to Tina.

SATURDAY 15

Birthday of Sarah, Duchess of York

SUNDAY 16

Atone (n.): to make amends
Mia had to atone for the wrong she'd done Lana via the nutty royale by paying Lana's cheerleading sweater dry-cleaning bill.

Random Act of Princess

Write a poem incorporating something you're learning in school.
        Columbus sailed the ocean blue
            in fourteen-hundred-ninety-two.
See how easy it is? Your poems are probably not as bad as you think, plus it makes remembering history that much easier.

October

MONDAY
17

TUESDAY
18
Mia receives her first kiss! Too bad it's from a frog, not a prince.

WEDNESDAY
19

THURSDAY
20
Baiser (n.): a kiss
Tante Simone expects Mia to give her un baiser on each cheek every time she visits.

FRIDAY

21

SATURDAY

22

SUNDAY

23

Time to start planning your Hallowe'en costume. Don't cheat and rent one either. Try to make one from objects and supplies found around the house.

Random Act of Princess

A princess never underestimates the importance of a kiss: practise when you can.

October

MONDAY
24

Princess Scorpio (24 October–22 November):
powerful, practical, loyal.
Nobody enjoys the throne more than you do,
Scorpio, what with all the sceptre-wielding.
Best royal consorts: Cancer, Pisces.
Possible brief affaires de coeur: Virgo, Capricorn.

TUESDAY
25

WEDNESDAY
26

THURSDAY
27

FRIDAY 28 — *Birthday of Crown Princess Sophie of Lichtenstein*

SATURDAY 29

SUNDAY 30 — *British Summer Time ends and the clock goes back*

Random Act of Princess

Hard up for costume ideas? Some easy and fun ones include:
- *Joan of Arc (use a rubbish-bin lid for your shield)*
- *Catwoman (wear a leotard and draw whiskers on with eyeliner)*
- *AOL Guy (yellow shirt, trousers)*

October

MONDAY
31

Hallowe'en (Remember to take your sweets to your local hospital to have them X-rayed if you live in an urban area.)

Helen Thermopolis and Frank Gianini's wedding anniversary.

Notes

November

Genovian Hallowe'en is celebrated on All Saints Day, 1 November.
It is traditional to wear a mask so the devil can't find you.

TUESDAY
1
All Saints Day
Diwali (Hindu)

WEDNESDAY
2
Sachet (n.): a small bag filled with a
sweet-smelling substance placed in wardrobe or
drawers
As she always uses her royal garden tea-rose
sachets, Grandmere's winter wools never smell of
mothballs.

THURSDAY
3
Eid-ul-Fitr (Muslim)

 November

FRIDAY *Birthday of Fat Louie*
4

SATURDAY *Bonfire Night*
5

SUNDAY
6

Random Act of Princess
If you live in a cool climate, it's probably time to put away your summer clothes. Use sachets to ward off any unpleasant odours. Even if you don't have your own royal garden from which to gather rose petals, you can make your own sachets: all you need is a sock and some cloves and cinnamon. Princessy!

MONDAY

7

Midterm grades will probably be coming out around now. Time to start asking your teachers for any extra credit projects.

TUESDAY

8

WEDNESDAY

9

Thwart (v.): to prevent a plan from being accomplished
Mia thwarted Kenny's amorous advances.

THURSDAY

10

FRIDAY
11
Remembrance Day, Canada

SATURDAY
12
Princess Marianne Day, Genovia
Get out your suit of armour and wear it all day
long the way Genovians do!

SUNDAY
13
Remembrance Sunday
In 1157, Princess Marianne thwarted a pirate
invasion of Genovia by dressing in a specially
made suit of armour and fighting them off.

Random Act of Princess

Time to brush up on your self-defence techniques! A princess
never depends solely on her bodyguard for protection. Enroll in
a local karate or kickboxing class. You'll burn calories and
learn ways to thwart your foes.

November

MONDAY

14

Only thirty-seven days left until Christmas/Hanukkah. Have you figured out what to get that special someone?

TUESDAY

15

Appreciate (v.): to be grateful for
Mlle Klein appreciated the crystal pomme from Tiffany that Mia left on her desk.

WEDNESDAY

16

THURSDAY

17

November

FRIDAY
18

SATURDAY *St Rainier's Day, Monaco*
19

SUNDAY
20

Random Act of Princess

As the autumn term gets closer to its end, it's a good idea to let your teachers know how much you appreciate them. Rare is the teacher who wouldn't enjoy receiving a sapphire cape clip or hat pin. (Apples work too.)

MONDAY
21

TUESDAY
22

WEDNESDAY
23

Princess Sagittarius (23 November
—23 December): progressive, giving, optimistic.
Who else do the people turn to in times of woe,
Sagittarius? You are depended upon.
Best royal consorts: Aries, Leo.
Possible brief affaires de coeur: Libra, Aquarius.

THURSDAY
24

Thanksgiving Day, USA
Be sure to take a moment to remember the many
Native Americans who have suffered under the
yoke of European oppression since the sixteenth
century. Mention this at the dinner table. Your
family will appreciate it.

FRIDAY

25

SATURDAY

26

Inevitable (adj.): tiresomely familiar
Inevitably, Mr G's dad tried to get Mia to eat
turkey on Thanksgiving.

SUNDAY

27

Dim sum at your favourite Chinese
restaurant (a favourite post-Thanksgiving
tradition in NYC)

Random Act of Princess

The holidays are a time for reconnecting with family members
you rarely see. Inevitably you will be asked, 'Do you have a
boyfriend?' Cut it off at the pass by loudly asserting that a
woman needs a man like a fish needs a bicycle. That will show
them.

MONDAY

28

TUESDAY

29

WEDNESDAY *St Andrew's Day*

30

On this day in 1964, the Beatles performed at the Royal Genovian Amphitheatre. They were not asked to return.

Notes

December

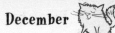

December brings all kinds of traditions and soirées celebrating the season. Be extra careful to write all your various plans down in this calendar lest you inadvertently double-book yourself.

Sometimes you can't help it if the Annual European Principality Carol Sing is scheduled on the same night as the local theatre's screening of the long-lost *STAR WARS* Christmas Special. If you can find a way to attend both, by all means do. Just don't let your host or date feel second best!

THURSDAY *Procession of the Fishing Boats, Genovia*

1

FRIDAY 2

Charitable (n.): generous

To be charitable, Mia likes to donate cans of Fancy Feast and nearly new cat toys to the local animal shelter.

SATURDAY 3

Lighting of the Courthouse Christmas Tree, Versailles, Indiana

SUNDAY 4

Random Act of Princess

December is the month for giving. A princess never forgets to give to the less fortunate, and you don't need to donate money to be charitable. Donate your time to a local homeless shelter, hospital or library. You will fully be the envy of your friends and your karma will rock as well.

MONDAY

5

Time to slip into high gear with the extra credit thing. Offer to write thousand-word essays on a variety of topics, including ice-worms, Asperger's syndrome and the environmental ramifications of deforestation.

TUESDAY

6

WEDNESDAY

7

THURSDAY

8

Gift vouchers from a local bookshop make a thoughtful present.

FRIDAY
9

List (n.): inventory, catalogue of names or words

Creating lists makes Mia feel organized and in control

SATURDAY
10

SUNDAY
11

Random Act of Princess

Time to start making that list and checking it twice:

Mum:	*Cat/Dog/Pony:*
Dad:	*Best Friend:*
Brother/Sister:	*Second Best Friend:*
Grandmere:	*Royal Consort:*

MONDAY
12
Modest (adj.): humble
Fat Louie doesn't mind modest presents — as long
as they involve catmint.

TUESDAY
13

WEDNESDAY
14

THURSDAY
15
It's never too early to start dropping
hints to the royal consort that a piece of modest
jewellery would be preferable to, say, a sweater or
a stuffed animal of some sort.

FRIDAY
16
Check with the royal secretary to see how the season's-greetings cards are coming along. If you don't have a royal secretary, start licking.

SATURDAY
17

SUNDAY
18

Random Act of Princess

Running low on cash? Some charming and easy-to-make gifts include:
- *Home-made stationery: Take pieces of white paper and stamp each page with an image carved on a potato. Pretty!*
- *Bird-feeder: Find a pine cone. Coat it with peanut butter. Roll it in sunflower seeds. Perfect!*
- *Cat toy: Fill a sock with catmint. Give it to your cat, but be sure to tie up the open end first!*

MONDAY *Anniversary of Mia's first kiss with Michael*

19

TUESDAY

20

WEDNESDAY *Winter solstice*
Shortest day of the year. To ward off seasonal
depression from lack of UV rays, schedule a
viewing of CAPTAIN RON.

21

THURSDAY *Princess Capricorn (22 December–20*
January): ambitious, confident, lively.
Will your kingdom triumph? With you on the
throne, Capricorn, success is certain.
Best royal consorts: Taurus, Virgo.
Possible brief affaires de coeur: Scorpio, Pisces.

22

FRIDAY
23
Disappoint (v.): Failure to fulfil expectations
Though Rocky only got Mia a screen saver with pictures of himself for Christmas, Mia was not disappointed by his gift.

SATURDAY
24
Christmas Eve

SUNDAY
25
Christmas Day
Hanukkah begins at sundown

Random Act of Princess

A princess never expresses disappointment in a gift, especially not to the giver. If a royal consort fails to come through with that perfect something, never let him know you have no use for that 2 FAST 2 FURIOUS DVD. Instead, start hinting now about that charm bracelet or necklace for Valentine's Day.

December

MONDAY *Boxing Day*

26

TUESDAY _UK Bank Holiday_

27
Start lining up (if you haven't already) that all-important New Year's Party, unless you plan on staying in and celebrating the big night with a James Bond movie marathon.

WEDNESDAY

28

THURSDAY

29

FRIDAY 30
Sans (prep.): without
Don't forget the cherry ChapStick for that kiss at midnight (or the microwave popcorn if you're celebrating sans consort).

SATURDAY 31
New Year's Eve

SUNDAY 1
Happy New Year 2006!!!!!!!

Random Act of Princess
Congratulations! You made it through another year. Give yourself a royal curtsy and get ready to start all over again...

Top Ten Best Moments of 2005

1. _____
2. _____
3. _____
4. _____
5. _____
6. _____
7. _____
8. _____
9. _____
10. _____

Comments: _____

_____
_____
_____
_____
_____
_____
_____
_____

Important Addresses and Telephone Numbers

Name: Emily Stoker

Address: 7 Peanwood Close, Tarporley, Cheshire, CW6, 0UF

Phone number: 01829 73297 Email:

Name: Charlotte Edgehill - Crump

Address: The corner house,

Phone number: 01829 733743 Email:

Name: Sophie Johnson

Address: 1 the greenwood

Phone number: 732240 Email:

Name:

Address:

Phone Number: Email:

Name:

Address:

Phone number: Email:

Important Addresses and Telephone Numbers

Name: _____

Address: _____

_____

Phone number: _____ Email: _____

Name: _____

Address: _____

_____

Phone number: _____ Email: _____

Name: _____

Address: _____

_____

Phone number: _____ Email: _____

Name: _____

Address: _____

_____

Phone Number: _____ Email: _____

Name: _____

Address: _____

_____

Phone number: _____ Email: _____

My Resolutions for 2006

1. _____
2. _____
3. _____
4. _____
5. _____
6. _____
7. _____
8. _____
9. _____
10. _____

Comments: _____

_____

_____

_____

_____

_____

_____

_____

Important Dates in 2006

Top Ten Celebs I'd Invite to stay in My Palace if I Were a Princess

1. _____
2. _____
3. _____
4. _____
5. _____
6. _____
7. _____
8. _____
9. _____
10. _____

Comments: _____

_____

_____

_____

_____

_____

_____

_____

Top Ten Laws I'd Pass if I Were a Princess

1. _____
2. _____
3. _____
4. _____
5. _____
6. _____
7. _____
8. _____
9. _____
10. _____

Comments: _____
_____
_____
_____
_____
_____
_____
_____

Lilly   Mia   Michael

Lars   Grandmere   Josh

Prince Phillippe   Paolo   Hank

Shameeka

Kenny

Tina

René

Sebastiano

Lana

Fat Louie

MEG CABOT

The
PRINCESS
DIARIES

What readers said about Meg Cabot's
The Princess Diaries 1 to 3:

"I love your books *The Princess Diaries*. I need to know how I can contact Amelia Thermopolis. I want to chat with her."

Brandi

"Mia is such an awesome character. All I want to say is keep up the good work so people like me can continue to read your books and dream of being a princess."

Maggie, 13

"You probably think I am nothing like Mia – but it's incredible how when I read the first *Princess Diaries* book, I thought it had been written about me! We're identical – apart from the whole princess thing."

Rachel, 12

"I love *The Princess Diaries* and the movie. I laughed out loud tons of times at it and annoyed my sister."

Lindsay

MEG CABOT

All American Girl

*Just as a general thing, when you have saved the life of the
leader of the free world, most people really want to hear about
that, and, sadly, don't care to hear a long-winded description
of your dog.*

Sam Madison's life used to be simple – if boring.
After all, it's not much fun being the totally forgotten
middle sister between a perfect, beautiful older one
(Lucy) and a genius, precocious younger one (Rebecca).
And then there's the weird art class Sam's been made
to attend. Er, hello, what is *that* all about?

But then comes the day that changes everything – when
Sam stops a crazy psycho from assassinating the President
of the United States and becomes an instant, world-
famous, full-on celebrity. Dining at the White House sure
isn't easy for someone who only eats hamburgers and
fries, and who lives in combat boots.

In fact, there's only one compensation – David the
President's son . . .

Discover your inner princess!

The PRINCESS DIARIES

Guide to Life

Meg Cabot

The PRINCESS DIARIES Princess Club

HEY, PRINCESS,
WANNA JOIN THE PRINCESS DIARIES PRINCESS CLUB?

4 fantastic comps and regular doses of fashion, gossip and games direct 2 ur mobile txt ur date of birth (dd,mm,yy)

to **07950 080700**

You will also get FREE unpublished snippets, exclusive games & comps!

08,11,91